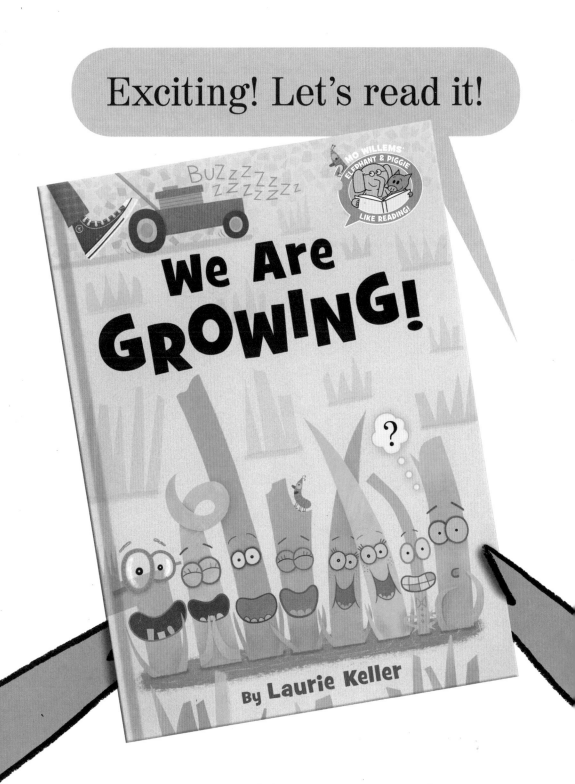

An **ELEPHANT & PIGGIE LIKE READING!** Book

Hyperion Books for Children / *New York*

AN IMPRINT OF DISNEY BOOK GROUP

To growing readers everywhere!

And, wheelbarrows of thanks to Mo Willems and
Tracey Keevan. It was so mulch fun working with you.

First Edition, September 2016
1 3 5 7 9 10 8 6 4 2
FAC-019817-16152
Printed in Malaysia
Reinforced binding

Library of Congress Cataloging-in-Publication Data
Names: Willems, Mo, author, illustrator. | Keller, Laurie, author, illustrator. Title: We are growing!
by [Mo Willems and] Laurie Keller. Description: Los Angeles ; New York : Hyperion Books for
Children, an imprint of Disney Book Group, [2016] | Series: Elephant & Piggie like reading!
| Summary: "Walt is not the tallest or the curliest or the pointiest or even the crunchiest. A
confounded blade of grass searches for his 'est' in this hilarious story about growing up"—Provided
by publisher. Identifiers: LCCN 2015042555 | ISBN 9781484726358 (hardback) Subjects: | CYAC:
Growth—Fiction. | Grasses—Fiction. | Humorous stories. | BISAC: JUVENILE FICTION / Concepts /
General. | JUVENILE FICTION / Humorous Stories. | JUVENILE FICTION / Social Issues / Values &
Virtues. Classification: LCC PZ7.W65535 Wd 2016 | DDC [E]—dc23
LC record available at http://lccn.loc.gov/2015042555

Visit hyperionbooksforchildren.com
and pigeonpresents.com

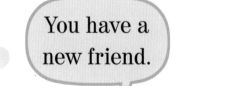

4

I know, I know.
I made it look
EASY.

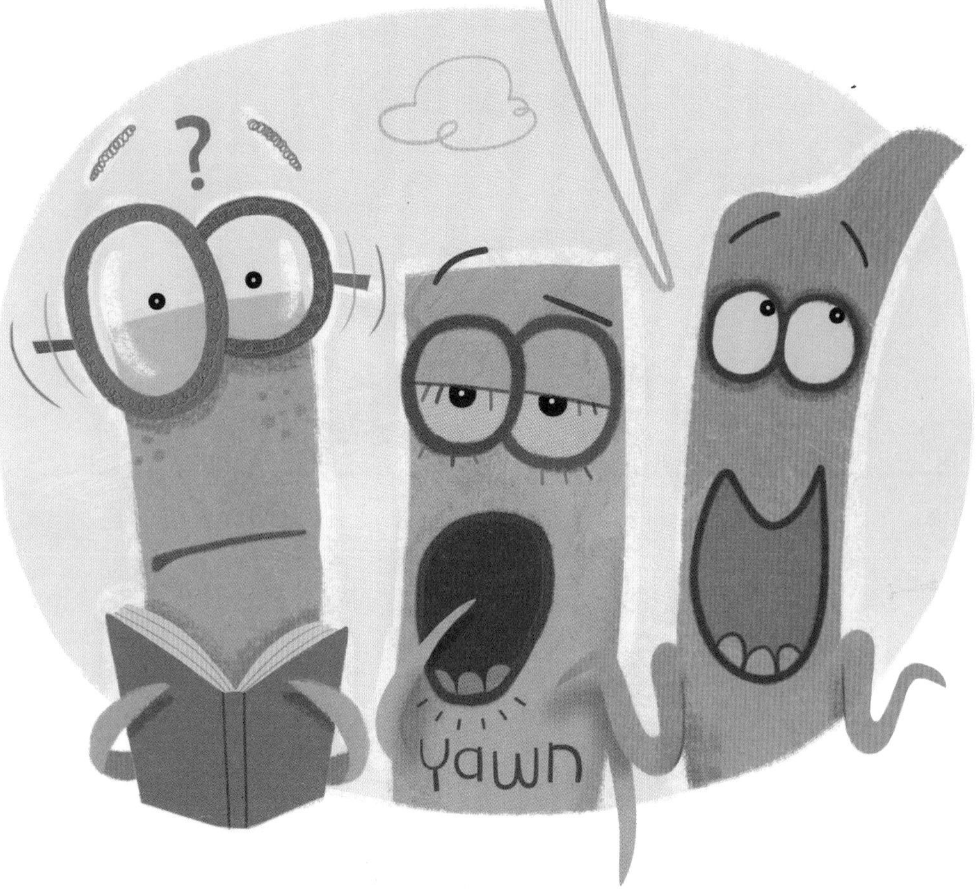

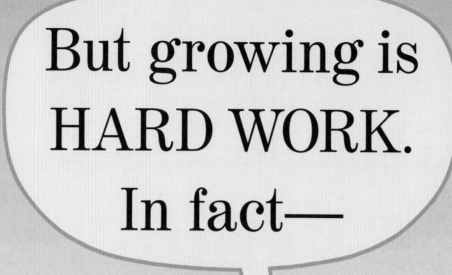

10

11

You are growing TALL.

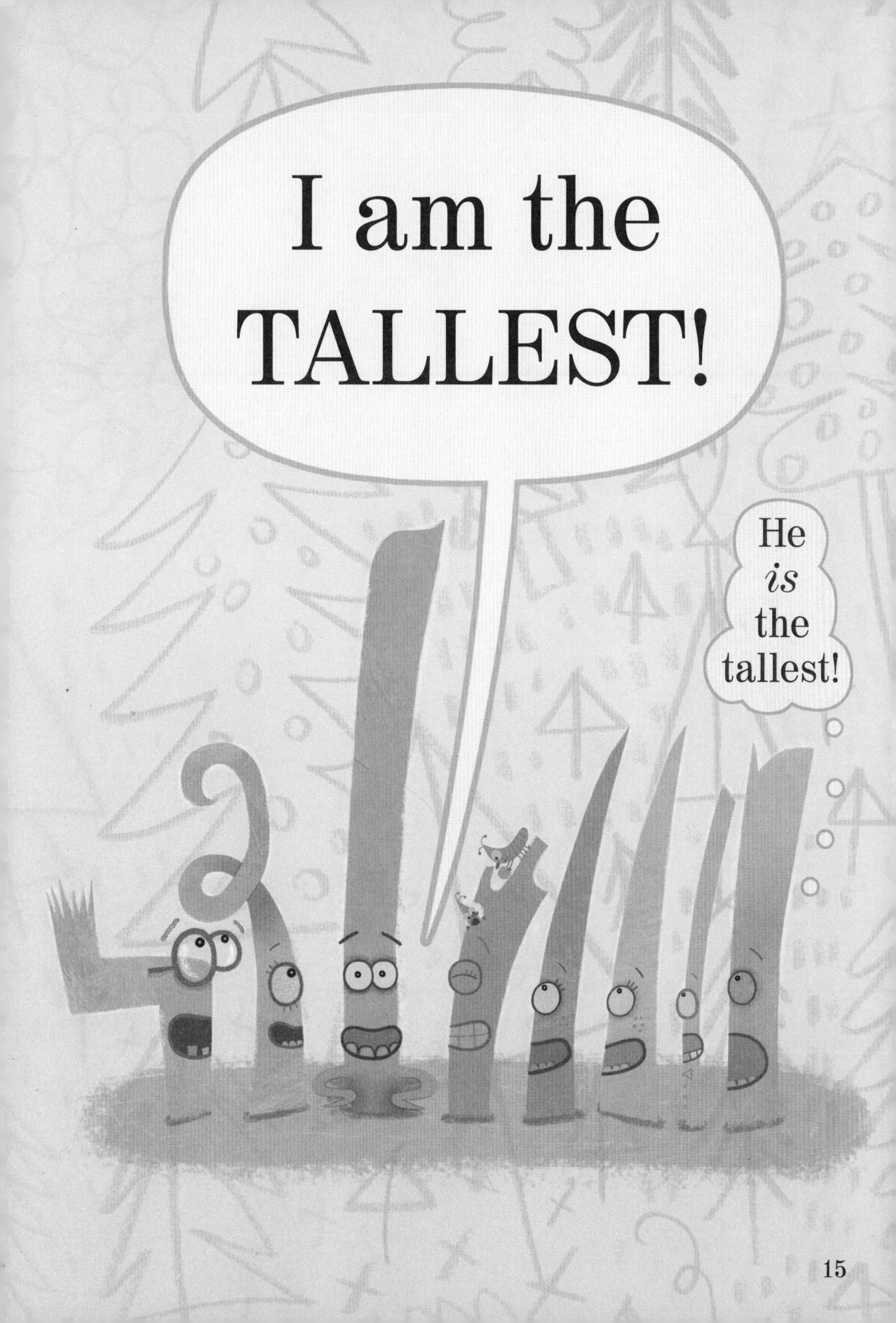
I am the TALLEST!
He *is* the tallest!

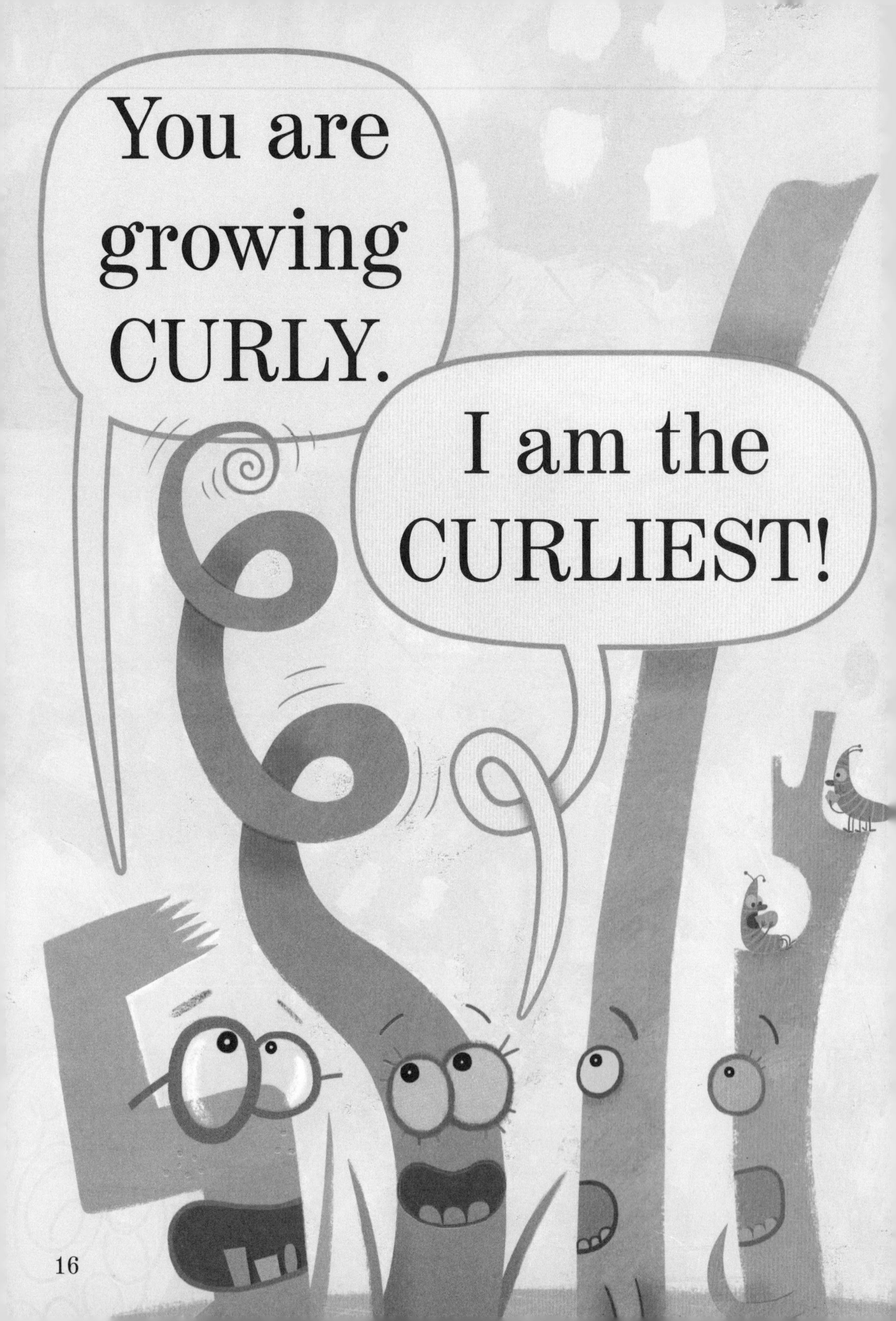
You are growing CURLY.
I am the CURLIEST!

18

POP!

I am the DANDIEST!

Well... I am not the *TALLEST*

or the *CURLIEST*

or the *SILLIEST*

or the *POINTIEST*

or the *CRUNCHIEST*

or the *DANDIEST.*

23

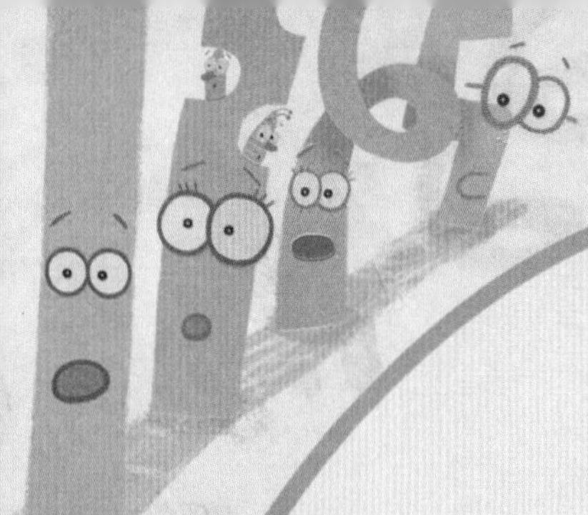

I do not know *WHAT* I am!

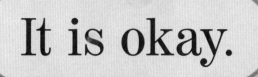

29

31

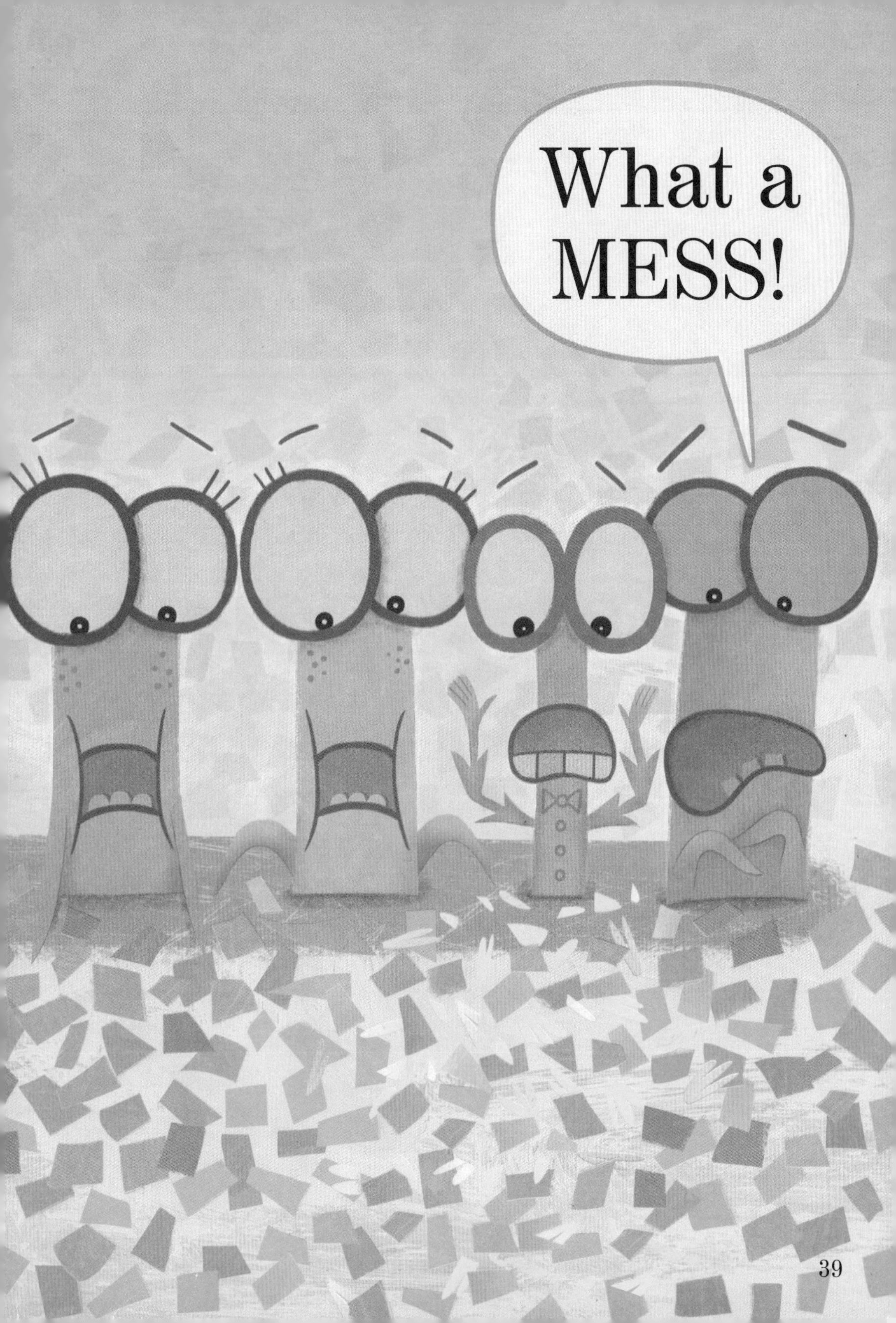
What a MESS!

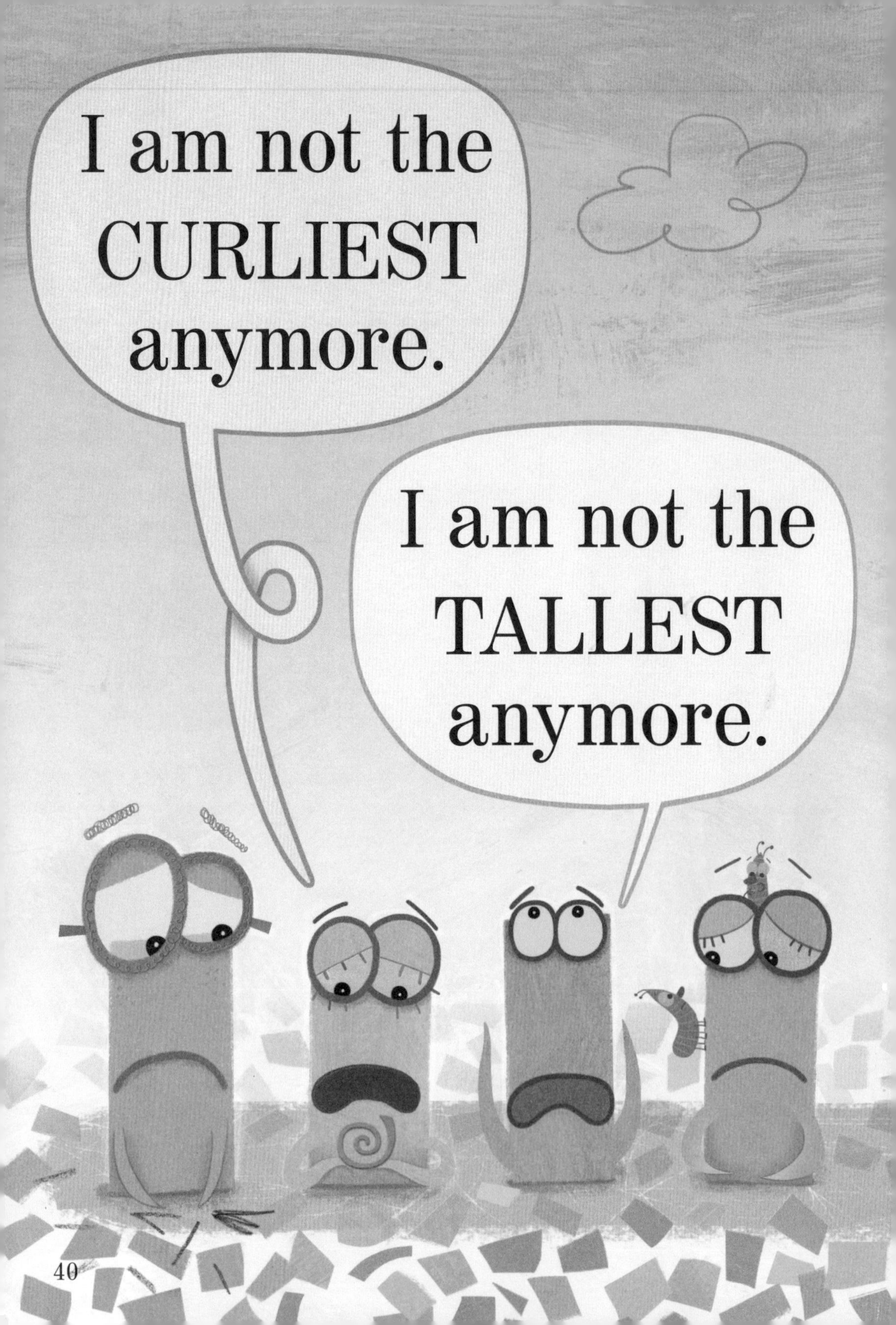
I am not the CURLIEST anymore.
I am not the TALLEST anymore.

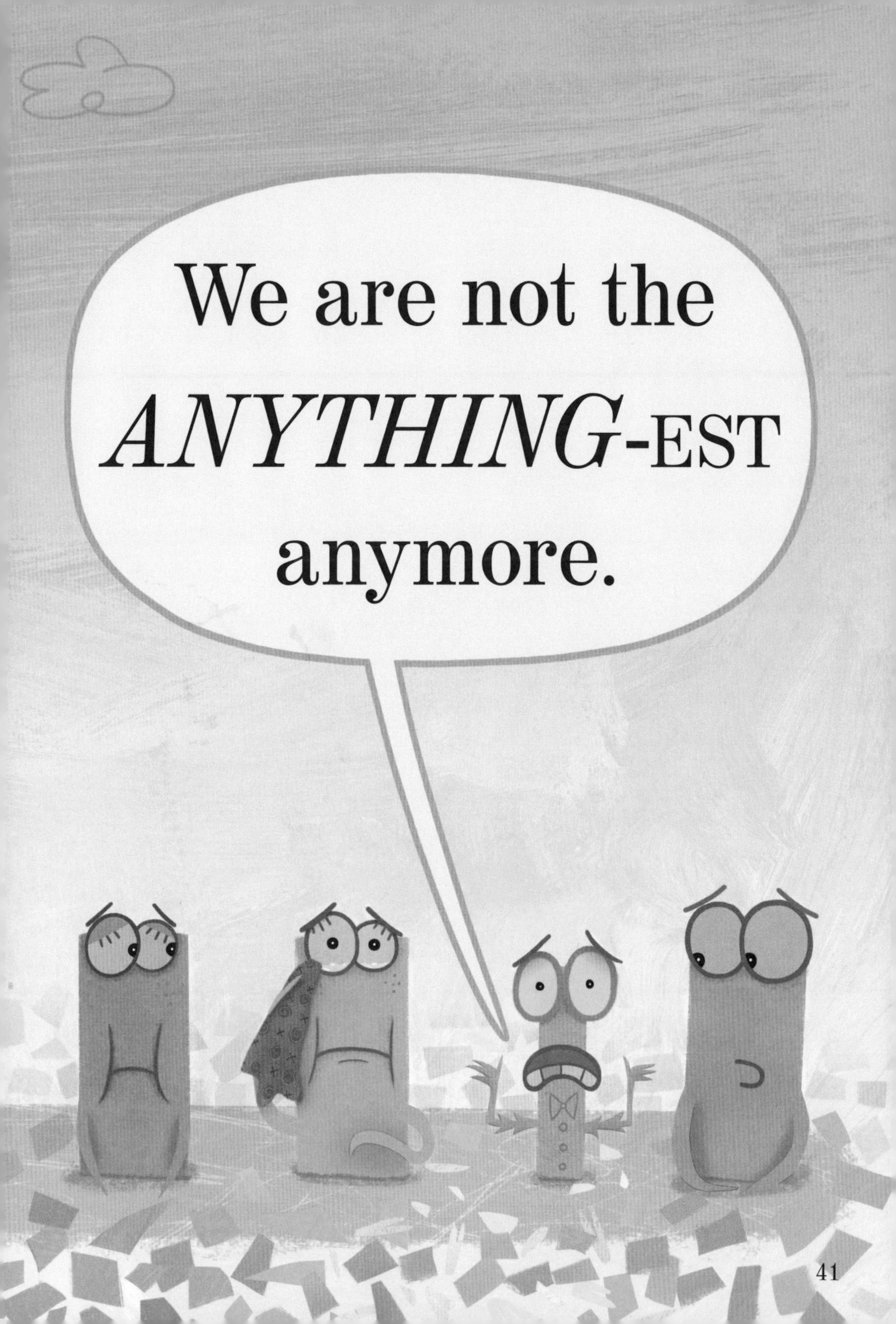
We are not the *ANYTHING*-EST anymore.

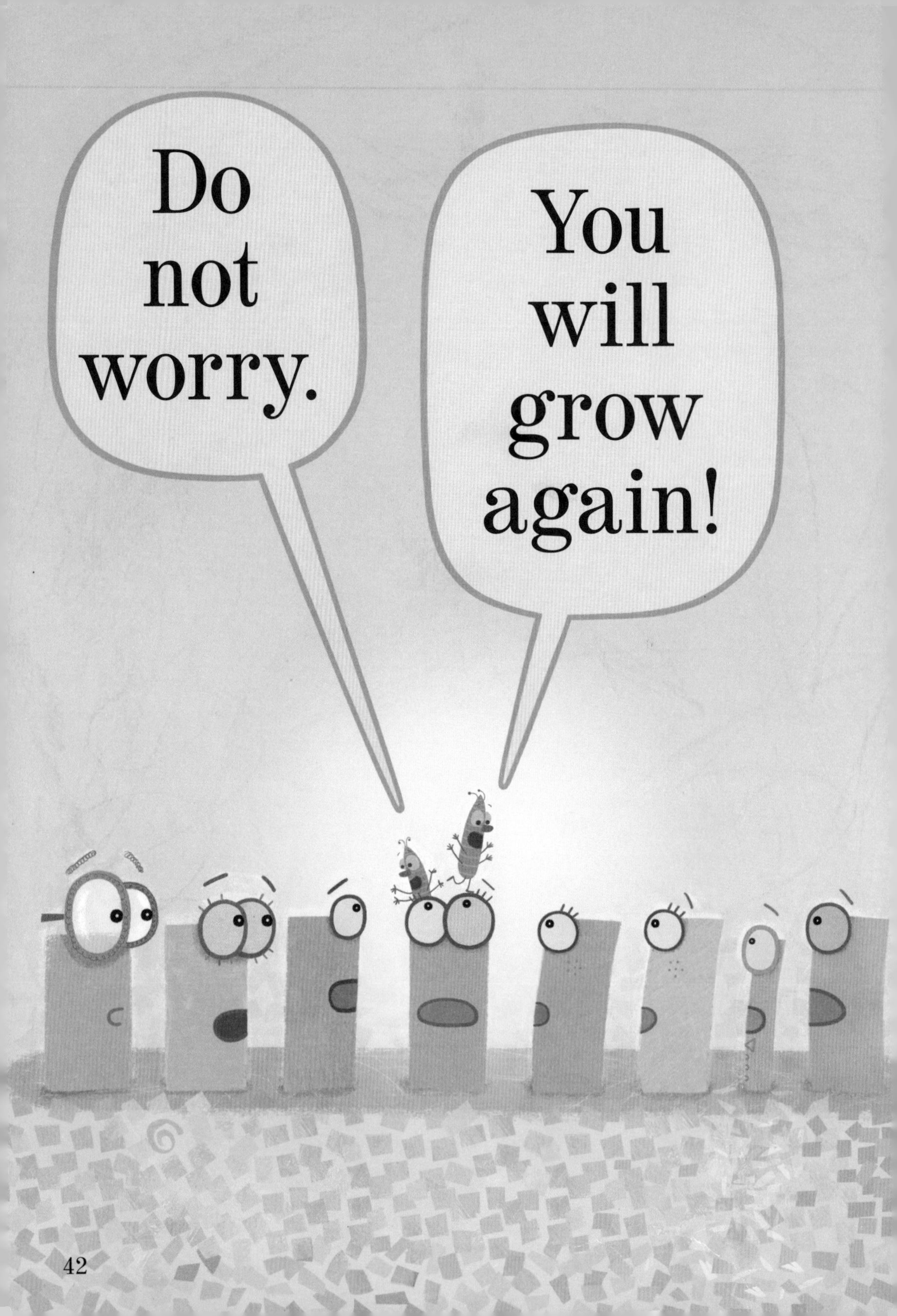
Do not worry.
You will grow again!

43

Before we grow, let's clean this place up.

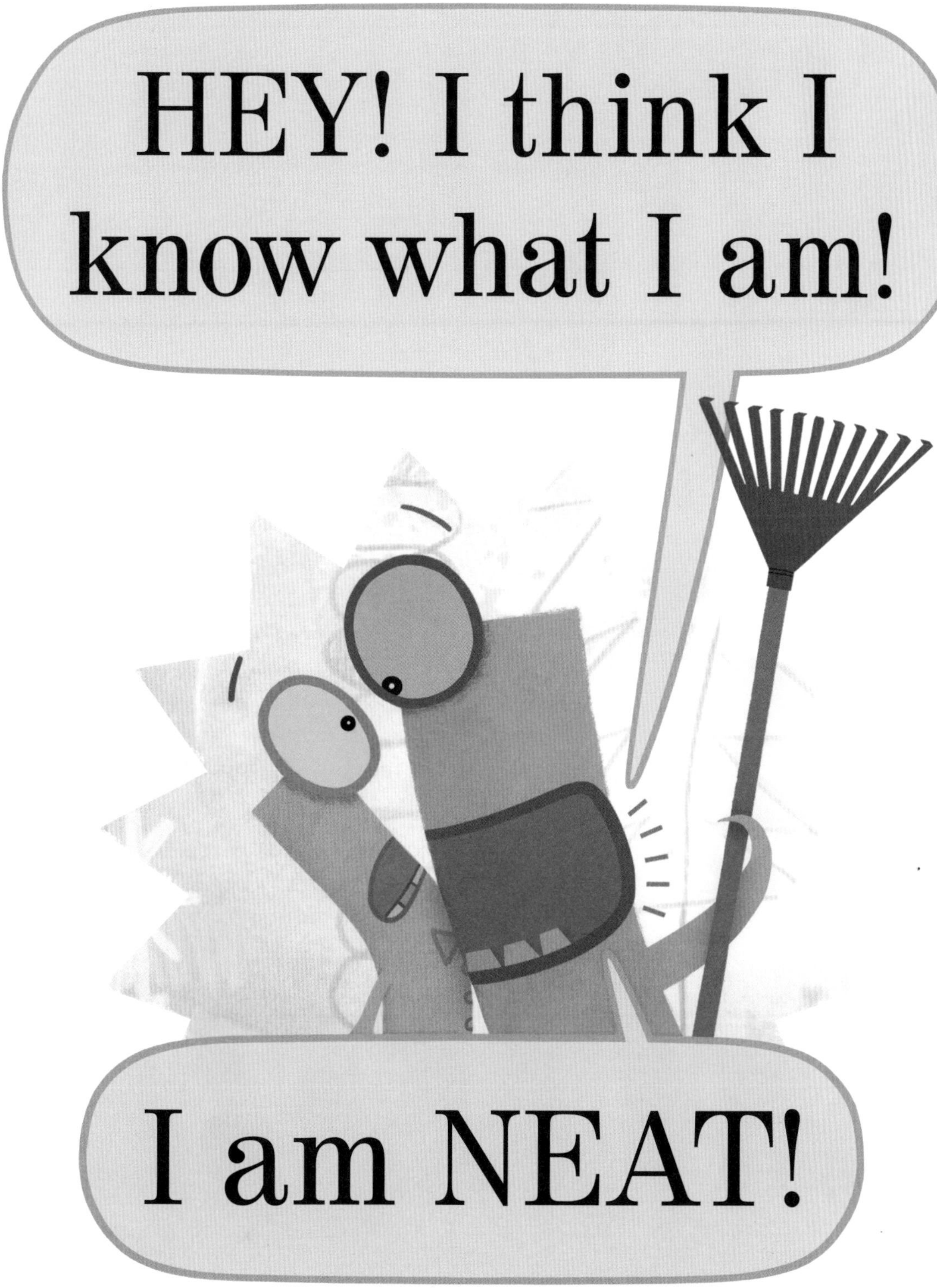
HEY! I think I know what I am!
I am NEAT!

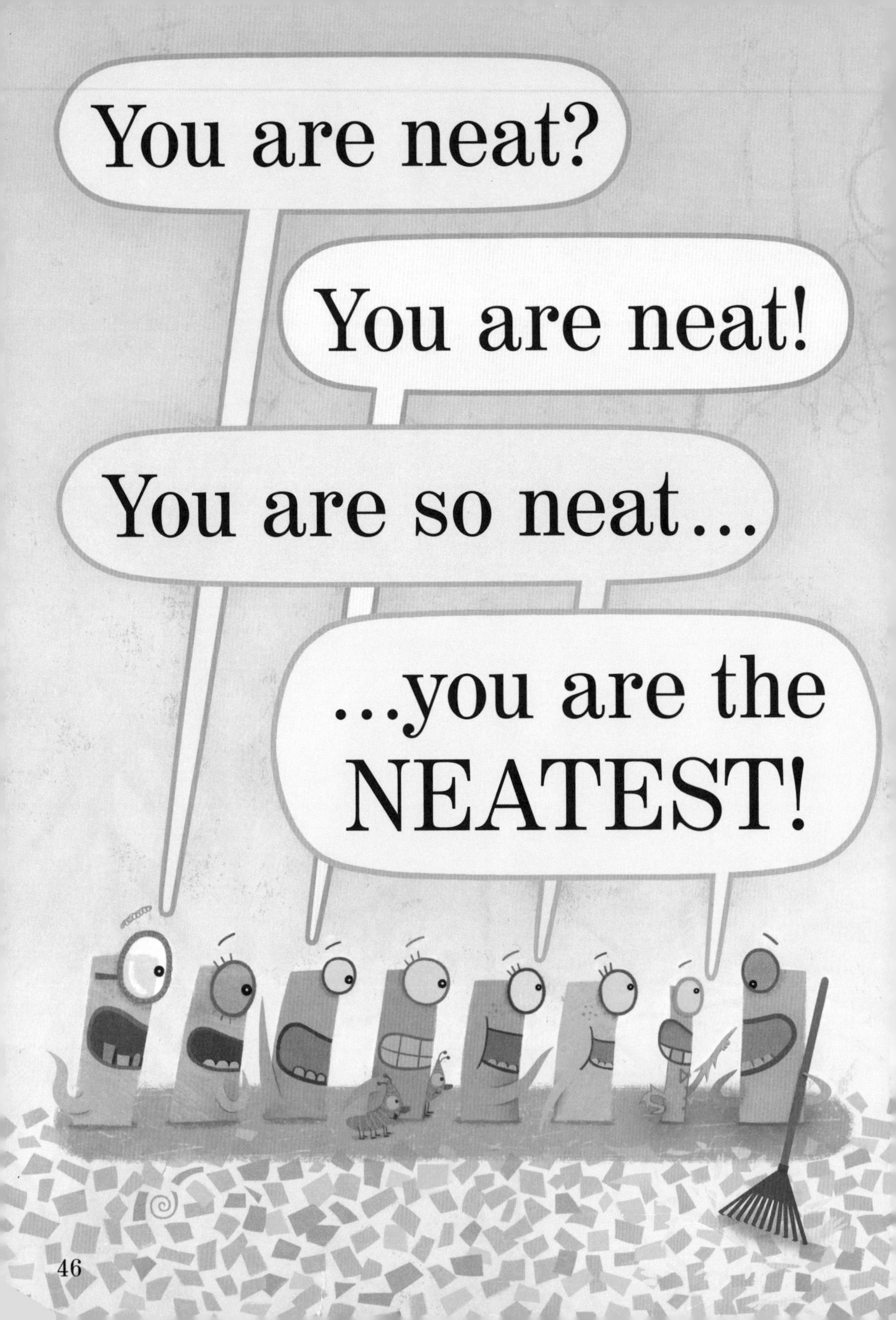
You are neat?
You are neat!
You are so neat...
...you are the NEATEST!

We are ALL the *SOMETHING*-EST!